Virgilio García

INVASION BY PENN AND VENABLES

Naval battle against the pirates
of the Caribbean

INVASION BY PENN AND VENABLES
Naval battle against the pirates of the Caribbean

Invasion by Penn and Venables is a work of fiction inspired by historical facts that happened in La Española in the seventeenth century. Names, characters, places and incidents either are the product of the author's imagination or have been used fictitiously.

ISBN-13: 978-0692383216
ISBN-10: 0692383212

Published in United States by
Quisqueya USA
1050 W 49th St. # 28043
Hialeah, FL 33012
QuisqueyaUSA@QuisqueyaUSA.net

DEDICATION

I dedicate this book to my parents,
my lovely wife Vilma, to my daughter Michelle,
and my son César. Also to my grandchildren,
Leilani, Kaytlyn, Jade, Victoria, Arelys, and
César Xavier

Preface

In 1654, the UK Protector, Oliver Cromwell, orchestrated a plan to conquer the rich territories of America possessed by Spain, especially the colony of Cartagena, the Viceroyalty of Peru and the Mexican Empire. Cromwell also wanted to have complete control of the Caribbean's seaways; these were used to transport precious metals, goods and African slaves. For the first stage of his ambitious project, the dictator ordered the navy to invade La Espanola. The navy, sent to the shores of Santo Domingo, comprised 56 warships, armed with 1,100 and 10,800 infantrymen. Never before had Great Britain ordered a military invasion of such magnitude.

After two weeks of bombing, sieges and battles, the Spanish colony of Santo Domingo— who at that time had only 500 soldiers, aided by 200 brave Creoles— withstood the onslaughts of the most powerful naval armada in the world. On May 5, 1655, the generals who commanded the invasion, Generals Penn and Venables, weighed anchor— this was the most dishonorable defeat suffered by the British Empire and its ruler, Oliver Cromwell.

These historical accounts inspired this story. We discovered the occurrences of supernatural phenomena; encounters with pirates; the existence of super-warriors, Indians and Creoles— all in search of an explanation for this unprecedented military defeat in the seventeenth century. I hope that reading this story is to your liking.

Virgilio García

Peace of Westphalia

In the towns of Munster and Osnabruck, located the historic Westphalia region west of Germany, between January and October 1648, a series of treaties known as the Peace of Westphalia were signed. The main participants were France, Spain, Sweden, the Netherlands (better known as Holland), Switzerland and the Holy Roman Empire, which included Hungary, Germany, Austria and Bohemia. The pact was a series of agreements between countries which for years fought wars for territorial, political or religious reasons.

The Peace of Westphalia is considered a pact unparalleled in the history of civilization, because never before had anyone managed to reconcile so many nations and to end many wars at once. From the religious point of view the Peace of Westphalia represented a blow to Catholicism, to the point that the Papal Nuncio of the city of Munster refused to sign the treaty, and even Pope Innocent X declared it "null and illegal"— none of the signatory countries heeded the decision of the Pontiff.

From this date would cease the prosperous influence of Catholicism in Europe; in turn Protestantism flourished, especially in Germany and England. Moreover the Westphalia's agreements would result in a new political-economic order in Europe. Among other things, Germany ended an internal war held over the course of 30 years, which left the country divided into about 60 regions and economically very weak.

The agreements were substantial; we list here what we consider the most significant:

1. The power of the Holy Roman Empire was significantly decreased, because independence was granted to numerous German principalities, while the nascent empire of Austria and Hungary was recognized as an autonomous entity.

2. Switzerland was recognized as an independent country.

3. Sweden acquired the cities of Wismar and Stettin conjointly with the territories of Bremen and Verden.

4. France expanded its borders and takes over the rich territories of Toul and Breisah, both irrigated by the river Rhine.

5. Spain ended a war that had been held for eighty years and gave freedom to the Netherlands, while recognizing all its conquered territories.

Spain and the Holy Roman Empire bore the brunt of the agreements, whereas the most favored were Switzerland, the Netherlands and France. By this time Spain had already granted freedom to Portugal, so that the Iberian Peninsula was divided into two countries— Spain's power was significantly reduced because the Netherlands' independence. England, although not involved in Westphalia, was indirectly well favored, especially because of internal conflicts in France and the deterioration of Spanish power. The new powers of Europe would be Holland, France and England.

With the industrialization of the Old Continent and the development of a middle class called "wealthy bourgeoisie", a great demand for raw material emerged in Europe, mainly for leather, cotton, wood, precious metals such as gold and silver, spices, tobacco and sugar. This increased demand, coupled with a shortage of habitable land in Europe, is what motivated the rising powers to conquer new territories in America.

Since independence from the Netherlands, the inspired Dutch, who already possessed the most powerful naval armada of the time, continued its offshore gains, especially in the Caribbean. In the West Indies they already possessed the islands of Aruba, Curacao, Bonaire and St. Martin, and had colonized part of the west coast of Africa. In the American continental territory, they also owned New Amsterdam, which is today New York, and the entire southern territory of the Guianas.

After the discovery of the New World, the new European powers used an unusual conquest method to allow merchants to colonize territories overseas on behalf of their flag country. It turned out, for example, that many of the achievements on behalf of the Netherlands were conducted by a private company called the Dutch Company of the West Indies. Canada managed to colonize the French part of the west coast of Africa and the Caribbean islands, including Martinique and Guadeloupe, by financing merchant shipping companies. The English East India Company financed the conquest of the Windward Islands, St. Kitts and Nevis on behalf of Britain.

Oliver Cromwell

Oliver Cromwell was born on April 25, 1599 in Huntingdon, located in the region of East Anglia in England. His parents, Robert Cromwell and Elizabeth Steward, came from Protestant families. From his early educational training Cromwell was heavily influenced by the religious fervor of his parents; years later he became a champion of the anti-Catholic puritanism of the time. He was educated at Cambridge and studied law in London. At the age of twenty-nine he was elected as Member of Parliament representing his hometown. His participation was short-lived, however, because a year later King Charles I dissolved parliament and managed to govern without legislators for eleven years. But social pressures were so many that the king had to yield for a new parliament elect.

In 1640, Cromwell was reelected to the English parliament, this time with much greater political maturity, and had become the leader of the opposition to the ruling monarchy. In November 1641 the new parliament submitted to King Charles I for constitutional reform. This was rejected by the king, causing heavy fighting with most of the population. Conflicts between king and parliament worsened rapidly which eventually led to the first civil war in England.

Two powerful fronts were involved in one of the bloodiest conflicts in the history of Britain. One side was the monarchy, which had the support of the wealthy and the Church of England, with its believers in the government of Divine Providence. On the other side were the Parliamentarians, with the support of the middle class, the poor, the Calvinist Puritans and those who opposed a strong monarchy.

In 1642, Cromwell submitted a petition to parliament to allow him, as a member of the legislature, to enlist in the military. Oliver was convinced it was his duty to defend his region of the intolerant monarchy, but also believed that a member of parliament should have good military training. His request was approved and he enlisted in the fighting force called Parliamentary Militia.

The great military leadership of Oliver Cromwell helped him to reach, in just two years, the positions of captain (Battle of Edgehill, October 1642), colonel (Battle of Gainsborough, July 1643), and lieutenant general (Battle of Marston Moor, July 1644) . In January 1646, the first civil war ended, but in January 1648 the second civil war began, this time against the territories of Ireland and Scotland.

Ireland had been under the control of the Irish Confederate Catholics, who had signed an alliance with the leadership of the British Royal political party. For the next fifty-four months Britain, Scotland and Ireland were immersed in a cruel and bloody war in which terrible massacres of innocent people occurred.

Cromwell's forces defeated the Coalition and the Royals. At one of the military incursions, Cromwell met a British army officer named Robert Venables who, years later, would be entrusted to one of the most ambitious military projects record the history of Britain.

On September 3, 1650, Oliver Cromwell, as Commander in Chief of the British army, crushed the armed forces of the Scottish King Charles II at the Battle of Worcester, effectively ending the Second English civil war. For the next ten years, the existence of kings would cease in England— this period in history is known as "Between Kings". Power between parliament and Cromwell was shared, but in actuality Cromwell was the ruler. He was able to give the approval for a series of harsh penal laws against the Catholic Church, as well as the legal authority to confiscate Ireland.

The conquest of Ireland was extremely brutal, to the point that even today it is the subject of controversial debates, nationally and internationally, whether Cromwell should be regarded as a national hero or as a cruel dictator who should had been tried for horrendous war crimes and even genocide.

Control of the English Channel

By 1651, the Netherlands and Britain were in dispute over the control of the English Channel, specifically the maritime portion that separates the south-eastern part of the British islands and Europe. Strategically speaking, this channel was extraordinarily important because of its geographic location. All vessels destined for London, Paris, Amsterdam or even the coastal ports of Germany had to make the journey across the English Channel. The Dutch advocated the principle of "open mare"— that is, the free marketing and transportation of products by all seas— but the British did not share this practice as they had always been considered by the world, and considered themselves, to be the "Lords of the Seas".

Oliver Cromwell, who, besides being a great military strategist, was also a political brain. In mid-1651, after months of negotiations, alliances and agreements, he achieved a constitutional reform that included, among other things, that the English Parliament enact a law or Act of Navigation. This law required that all goods imported to Britain should be transported on British ships, and furthermore demanded that all vessels, regardless of country of origin, must have their flags at half-mast to show respect whenever they encountered a British ship.

These measures infuriated the Dutch, who had already become one of the most powerful naval powers of the time. There are records of conflicts between the English and the Dutch since 1623 in which the Dutch massacred the inhabitants of the British-owned lands of Bosnia and Amboina in southern India. From mid-1651 until 1653 there was a series of naval battles between the Dutch and the English, in which the Dutch rule was imposed because they were excellent sailors and their naval armada was much bigger than the English, although the British were more disciplined.

In November 1652, the British naval armada suffered a crushing defeat by the Dutch in the Battle of Dungeness, led by the great Dutch Admiral Tromp. After the humiliating defeat, the British government took serious measures to avoid future defeats. The navy was subjected to a war council of officers who were in command of the battle, and a special committee was appointed to determine the specific causes of the defeat. One of the people who was part of this commission was Admiral William Penn who, at only thirty years old, was already part of the Royal Navy in England. Penn was an athletic man, about six feet three inches tall, who loved to read, and was a very smart person with vast nautical, historical and geographical knowledge.

Penn liked searching the scriptures of scholars and inventors, his favorites being Galileo, who invented the telescope; Kepler, who discovered the refraction of light; and Evangelista Torricelli, known as the father of modern meteorology. (Torricelli discovered the effects of pressure change on the layers of air over the land and the variation in wind movements. He also invented the barometer, an instrument used to measure the weight of the atmospheric layers above the ground).

The admiral had a natural instinct to predict the weather conditions of his environment. He acquired several powerful telescopes and barometers designed especially for him, and thus possessed the most modern navigation instruments of the time.

After examining some of the boats that participated in the defeat of Dungeness, Admiral Penn found that most of the guns on the British warships were misaligned and that many did not have the mobility to achieve optimum fire. Because of his great academic development and vast studies in geometry and physics, Penn knew that in order for the missile to reach the maximum distance, the optimum shooting angle should be about 45 degrees.

The admiral immediately ordered the readjustment of the guns, the inspection of the locations of the gunboats, and ordered special guns to be made. These guns were to be longer and narrower, and each vessel would have at least two in the bow and two in the stern. At the same time Penn organized training in the management of the naval guns because he was convinced that the defeat was caused by the mishandling of their main weapon of war— their cannons.

Towards the end of January 1653, the British naval armada had recovered. Several ships were repaired after the defeat of Dungeness, and many boats that had previously served as merchant ships were transformed to warships.

Naval Battle of Portland

In any competition or war there is always an event that is considered reaponsible for "changing the course", and the naval Battle of Portland in February 1653 was one of those events.

Portland is a small island of about six miles long and two wide, located south of the island of Great Britain. For two years the Dutch and the English had fought in several battles trying to gain control of the English Channel. After the Battle of Dungeness the Dutch believed themselves invincible. In early February 1653, the custody of some two hundred commercial vessels returning to Holland was entrusted to the Dutch Admiral Maarten Tromp. Tromp now had a strong naval contingent of about fifteen warships.

To the surprise of the Dutch admiral, on the morning of February 18, 1653, he found out that the British had sent near the coast of Portland, Oregon, three naval fronts, and each had five very well equipped warships. The fronts were White Front, Triomphe Front and Blue Front— the last commanded by Admiral William Penn.

The English admiral had sworn to defend the British honor because the Dutch's teasing included using dirty old brooms on their ships symbolizing the flag of Great Britain.

The English army was positioned south of the Dutch. The Dutch navy had the wind in their favor which Admiral Tromp took advantage of to attack the British. He first attacked the White Front. The excellent Dutch sailors were characterized by their aggressiveness in naval warfare. At the beginning of the battle, the Dutch inflicted heavy casualties on the British; they sunk one English ship and caused serious damage to three other warships. After such damage again the Dutch took advantage of having the wind in their favor and strategically maneuvered another group of Dutch ships to cause severe damage to the front Triomphe.

The White Front was in greater danger because one of its main craft had sunk and the Dutch had almost besieged another ship, whose marines, had mostly died or been thrown into the sea.

Penn was able to strategically approach so that the enemy guns did not have a chance to reach their boats; however, his special long-range guns began to bombard and knock down the main mast of the main sailboat of the greatest enemy ship. He immediately aimed his guns towards the center Dutch boat, causing heavy damage and a large fire, and after a while this boat began to sink.

The battle continued for several hours. Each engagement was characterized by the naval prowess of Admiral Penn, who was the real hero of the English victory in this battle known as the Battle of Portland, in which the Dutch suffered a crushing defeat. As a result, five boats were sunken, three severely damaged, four captured and about one hundred commercial vessels seized. Months later, after another two military encounters in which the Dutch were defeated, the war ended between the Dutch and the English and the British took complete control of the English Channel.

Cromwell, Lord Protector

After the British naval victories, Cromwell, being a prominent member of parliament, held the rank of Commander in Chief of the British Armed Forces and was considered a national hero. Cromwell and his helpers and counselors were not happy with how things were going in the legislative body and on April 20, 1653, the commander went to the parliament accompanied by two generals and a group of soldiers. He called the members of the parliment "corrupt"; "drunk"; "men without faith or moral", then, Cromwell proceeded to dissolve the parliament.

Cromwell directed his military subordinates to "choose" a new parliament, to consist of one hundred and forty men in England, five in Scotland and six in Ireland. On July 4, 1653, the new Commonwealth Parliament resigned completely, giving Cromwell absolute power without limits over the three nations: England, Ireland and Scotland. Cromwell appointed a state council composed of individuals he trusted. Months later, on December 16, 1653, the new state council gave to Cromwell the title of Lord Protector of the Commonwealth of England, Scotland and Ireland.

The title of Lord Protector was a special assignment given by the English Parliament if the king could not govern, whether by his minority or inability to perform his duties— as was the case of Richard Plantagenet being appointed Lord Protector of England between 1453 and 1455 due to the mental illness of Henry VI.

The Western Design

In mid-1653, the second edition of bestselling book *The English-American: a New Survey of the West Indies* was published in London, which was written in 1648 by former Irish Catholic priest Thomas Gage. Gage had traveled in 1625 as a missionary of the Order of the Dominicans in Santo Domingo. For about eleven years he lived in Mexico, Nicaragua and Darién, where he served many years of ministry with Central American Indians and was a true defender of the Indians. He was a very controversial priest who disagreed with celibacy and did not share many of the strict regulations that came from the Pope. In 1639 he hung his Catholic's habits, returned to England and converted to the Protestant religion, becoming one of the proponents of the anti-Catholic trend of the times.

Gage's book shows numerous detailed maps of the West Indies, Central America and what he describes as the rich and fascinating Mexican Empire. It likewise emphasize the huge deposits of precious minerals and excellent natural resources possessed by the Spanish colonies of America.

According to Gage, Spain was a country that, even though it had the honor of having discovered the New World, did not qualify as one of the European powers and therefore should not own the rich territories of America. He declared that all Spain's possessions in the New World should be owned by the most powerful country of the time in this case Britain. The book lashes out strongly against the Pope and the Catholic Church based on the fact that Spain had acquired the rich territories of America by a papal bull, and according to Gage, this fact made them complicit in all the abuses, crimes and atrocities committed against the defenseless Indians.

Thomas Gage's book, *The English-American: a New Survey of the West Indies*, impressed much of the Protestant community, and as a result the antipathy that already existed against Catholics increased significantly. Cromwell was no exception; many historians claim that Gage's writings inspired the project-conqueror named by Cromwel "The Western Design".

Cromwell visualized through this project the opportunity to "get even" with Spain because the Spanish reign never had allowed British free trade with America. He thought he could solve the serious economic situation faced by the country. On the other hand, Cromwell, like all good Puritans, and motivated by their religious fanaticism, thought he should move into war against the "slavish Catholicism" of the Spaniards. Considering all the above, the Protector planned the "Western Design" project with three main objectives.

Political / Military Purpose

Keeping the powerful British navy busy

Cromwell wished to maintain its military leadership so he decided to get involved in the military decisions of his army. On another note, some of his closest aides insisted that Spain, although weak could become very annoying, and was an enemy against whom he should declare war.

Spain had attacked the Caribbean Islands Saint Kitts and Nevis in 1629; and attacked the Providence islands in 1641. These attacks on the English colonies had Cromwell very annoyed; moreover, after having ended the war with Holland, the Protector had to keep his powerful naval fleet occupied.

With the conquest of the Spanish territories in America, Cromwell would avenge the Spaniards' attacks of his territories and could also extend his territorial empire westward. He could also impose his military strength, not only to control the trade routes, but to protect Britain's prosperous colonies in North America that included New England, Virginia, Maryland and the Province of Carolina.

Economic Purpose

To conquer the islands of the Greater Antilles, Perú and Mexico

According to Gage's book, the great riches of Peru and the Mexican Empire were indescribable; Cromwell was completely convinced that his new conquests could solve his country's economic problems. He was aware that the economy needed a big boost and firmly believed that from a commercial point of view, the ideal option was to export goods manufactured in England to all his colonies in exchange for raw materials or precious metals, but Spain did not allow England to trade with its colonies— this fact always angered the Protector.

On the other hand, the trade sale of African slaves had become an extremely lucrative business because of the great demand for slaves by the European colonies in America. Although England participated in this commercial practice, most of this market was controlled by the Dutch, Portuguese and French. The main route of transport of slaves to America was along the coasts of the Caribbean islands, which offered a naturally staggered approach so the vessels carrying any goods or slaves from Africa could acquire supplies or find shelter from the ravages of nature or enemy attacks.

Socio / Religious Purpose

Imposition of Protestantism as the official religion in America

This is the part of the project that was sold to the people and the opponents of Cromwell. He needed the people's support to bring out the anti-Catholicism of the time. The Protector proclaimed that God had chosen him to fight the evil Spaniards of America and that his war had the "divine" support to fight the injustices, abuses and crimes committed by the Catholic Spanish sinners of the New World.

The Protector never maintained good relations with the Spanish monarchy; firstly by his great antagonism towards everything that smelled Catholic, and secondly because Spain had always been supported by Holland. We must remember that the Netherlands were a Spanish colony until 1648 when they were recognized as an independent country after the Peace of Westphalia. Cromwell felt obliged to declare war on Spain— not in Europe because of the great political and economic costs, but in their possessions in the New World. Thomas Gage had convinced him of the Spanish military's weakness and felt sure it would be very easy to not only conquer Spain, but to impose Protestantism as the official religion in the New World.

Many military strategists have criticized the Cromwell's decision, because he did not appoint, from the beginning, a commander in chief of the expedition. Penn and Venables had similar powers and there was much rivalry between them. General Robert Venables felt very envious because Penn was ten years younger than him, and being so young he had already achieved the rank of General Admiral of the Royal Navy of England.

On December 24, 1654, the expedition, composed of eighteen warships and twenty transport ships, sailed from the port of Portsmouth in southern Britain. Here are the names of the warships with their respective captains and surcharges:

1. *Second Class Swiftsure*, 60 guns, 350 sailors and 30 soldiers, Flag Captain, Jonas Poole, General Admiral William Penn.

2. *Second Class Paragon*, 54 guns, 300 sailors and 30 soldiers, commanded by Vice Admiral William Good-son.

3. *Third Class Torrington*, 54 guns, 280 sailors and 30 soldiers, commanded by Admiral George Dakins.

4. *Third Class Marston Moor*, 54 guns, 280 sailors and 30 soldiers, led by Edward Blagg.

5. *Third Class Gloucester*, 54 guns, 280 sailors and 30 soldiers, led by Benjamin Blake.

6. *Third Class Lion*, 44 guns, 230 sailors and 30 soldiers, commanded by John Lambert.

7. *Third Class Mathias*, 44 guns, 200 sailors and 30 soldiers, led by John White.

8. *Third Class Indian*, 44 guns, 220 sailors and 30 soldiers, led by James Terry.

9.- *Fourth Class Rate Bear*, 36 guns, 150 sailors and 30 soldiers, commanded by Francis Kirby.

10. *Fourth Class Laurel*, 40 guns, 160 sailors and 30 soldiers, led by William Crispin.

11. *Fourth Class Portly*, 40 guns, 160 sailors and 30 soldiers, led by Richard Newberry.

12. *Fourth Class Dover*, 40 guns, 160 sailors and 30 soldiers, led by Robert Syers.

13. *Fourth Class Great Charity*, 36 guns, 150 sailors, led by Leonard Harris.

14. *Fourth Class Heartsease*, 30 guns, 70 sailors and 160 soldiers, led by Thomas Wright.

15. *Fourth Class Discovery*, 30 guns, 70 sailors and 160 soldiers, led by Thomas Wills.

16. *Fourth Class Convertine*, 30 guns, 75 sailors and 200 soldiers, led by John Hayward.

17. *Fourth Class Katherine*, 30 guns, 70 sailors and 200 soldiers, commanded by Willoughby Hannam.

18. *Fourth Class Martin*, 12 guns, 60 sailors, led by William Vesey.
(Data from Wikipedia.com)

The remaining twenty ships transported food, supplies and clothing, and also transported 1,145 sailors, 1,830 soldiers, 38 horses and 4 landing beach boats, all protected by 352 cannons. In short, a total of 42 boats, 1,084 guns, and 7,320 men. The above numbers show the magnitude of the expedition, which confirms the enormous interest that Cromwell had in this first phase of his ambitious conquering project.

During the next two weeks, the trip was very enjoyable; the boats traveled in "Y" formation and the sky was clear most of the time, sometimes overcast. The moderate winds blew westward or west-southwest, precisely in the direction marked on the map. The admiral's ship, *Second Class Swiftsure* always led the expedition. During the day the sailors and soldiers had a disciplined routine consisting maintenance of the sails, the ships and the combat teams; feeding the horses; fishing or cleaning the vessels—everyone was kept busy. After dinner they had fun participating in gatherings or improvised comedies in which they mocked everything that was not English, especially the Dutch and the French.

Even though they traveled in different ships, sometimes Penn and Venables cordially planned and agreed various aspects of the most important stage of the expedition: the invasion of La Española.

On the morning of January 18, 1655, the expedition had traveled more than half of the trip; their coordinates were: latitude 22.5 ° N, 47.5 ° W longitude. They were very close to where the imaginary lines of latitude, the Tropic of Cancer, and the 45 ° W meridian meet. In this specific geographical location in the Atlantic Ocean, implausible events have occurred since the history of navigation, including the disappearance of ships and all crew members, and other unexplained sinking of merchant fleets. Some legends suggest the existence of giant prehistoric animals in this mysterious area of the globe.

Admiral Penn awoke earlier than accustomed; he almost could not sleep and had spent much of the night awake, as if he had predicted that something dreadful would happen.

The first thing he did was go up to the deck and watch the horizon. He was mesmerized, he did not hear anything around himself. His gaze seemed to get lost in the distance where he imagined, the clouds were born from the depths of the seas, and as they moved up, the winds blew them in different directions. Suddenly, he turned to see flag captain beside him. He had already offered the regulatory salute, but the admiral had not responded because he was in "another world".

"Bring me the telescope," Captain Penn said to Jonas Poole.

"Here it is, Sir," said Jonas.

The admiral was contemplating, looking through his powerful yet small telescope toward the horizon and occasionally watching the movement of the clouds. He maintained this practice for about ten minutes without saying a word, then went to the desk in his dressing room where he kept some navigation instruments, including an impeccable barometer that shone as like a new Swiss watch.

After observing the barometric reading, he realized that the air pressure had dropped significantly. This fact disturbed him, and he returned in a hurry to the deck where he observed the waters and noticed a drastic change in the size of the waves as the wind began to blow with more intensity. He remained on deck as if trying to smell something. About fifteen minutes later, dark clouds covered the sky, which was until then completely clear. The southwestern horizon had lost its grayish blue hue to become a very dark gray.

After another ten minutes he glimpsed about two miles to the west an occurrence that looked as though all the clouds got together at a point in the sky and dropped down at high speed, surrounded by erratic thunder and lightning, forming a huge funnel to take the waters of the sea.

The frightened and curious crew went out on deck. Some soldiers said that a gigantic possessed elephant had lunged its huge trunk into the sea to drink all the water; others said that a crazy prehistoric snake had escaped from hell and was spinning on its axis at a high speed, swallowing everything it could find in its path.

Admiral Penn remained serene; he knew that a giant marine waterspout had formed with winds of 500 miles per hour and a diameter of about a mile. (This type of phenomenon is one of the most dangerous because, as the name implies, tornadoes on the sea surface usually form due to complex climatic fluctuations in warm waters, after a sudden drop in atmospheric pressure).

Despite all the suggestions, screaming and cries, Penn remained calm. A few minutes before, he had taken a final reading of the barometer and noticed a slight increase. He was on deck beside the helmsman and the flag captain; at the same time the winds were blowing faster with bursts of very fine rain, the waves increased in size and frequency, the sound of thunders was louder.

"WEST COURSE" Penn ordered.

The helmsman and flag captain were very astonished.

"West course?" exclaimed the helmsman, quite surprised because this was exactly the direction of the waterspout, which at that time had come very close to the ship. The thunder resounded with increasing threatening winds, illuminated by numerous lightning strikes.

"WEST COURSE," Penn repeated, raising his voice and staring at the captain, as he indicated to send the message to the rest of the ships.

Both the helmsman as the captain obeyed the order.

Robert Venables, who traveled in the rear of the fleet, knew the flag's language and as soon he was aware of Penn's orders said:

Venables: "Penn is crazy, cannot be as we will set sail towards the sea monster."

Venables: "Take southeast direction" Venables ordered William Goodson, the boat's captain.

The captain took a glance at Venables, who looked extremely worried. The atmosphere was dark, the waves continued to grow more stronger and beat the ships, the winds blew harder and the deafening noise of thunder was very annoying. Goodson did not know what to do, but he respected Admiral Penn's meteorological knowledge, and believed that Venables was right in refusing to go to the waterspout.

"I'll do what you say, but only if you assume full responsibility for all the consequences," responded Goodson.

"I am responsible for this issue and I take full responsibility for all the things that can happen from now on," replied Venables.

"HEADING SOUTH," shouted Goodson to his helmsman.

Only two ships did not obey Penn's order; one of them was Venables' ship. Admiral Penn remained very attentive to the meteor's movements so he did not notice the disobedience. A few minutes passed when an immense wave hit Penn's ship. The impact was such that one of the sailors was thrown into the sea— luckily he was saved by the heroic courage of two of his comrades, who rushed to his rescue and after secured him with strong ropes, them pulled him back on deck. The waves were hitting more fiercely. The frequent lightning strikes illuminated the area, followed by very loud thunders. The other ships had the same luck— it seemed as if they were being swallowed by the sea and approaching the end of the world. Everyone could see the frightful meteor before them. Suddenly, as if by magic, the storm began to recede and turned around 180 degrees, as if the storm was scared to see Admiral Penn's ship. After a few seconds the whirlwind took a south course and suddenly disappeared, leaving the sea calm, no lightning, no thunder— all with a heavenly tranquility.

Absolute silence. The only sound was a light wind caressing the candles. Everyone on deck had expressions of disbelief and astonishment, and reflected on the minutes of fear and despair that fate had given them.

"IT'S OVER! BACK TO WORK!" The Admiral Shouted. While ordering his subordinates to review the damages, Penn also ordered a count of all the ships on the expedition. Slowly all the sailors and soldiers returned to work.

Penn returned with his helmsman, Luis Manuel, both smiling and looking pleased that nothing disastrous had happened.

Luis Manuel: "With all due respect, why did you, Admiral, order to course west. Did you know the waterspout was going to change course?"

Penn: "These meteors are unpredictable but usually, once formed, tend to move away from the environment where the increased atmospheric pressure occurs. We lucked out."

Manuel Felipe: "You are a genius. I am very honored to be your helmsman."

Penn: "You are an excellent helmsman, Captain."

Two hours later the flag captain informed Admiral Penn that the ships were in "Y" formation, with the exception of the ships *Second Class Paragon and Fourth Class Martin*— the two ships that had disobeyed Penn's order. Both boats were gone. The admiral immediately climbed the central mast and with his powerful glasses slowly began tracking the horizon.

He searched for about thirty minutes and found nothing; the ships did not appear.

It seems the strong winds caused they lost their way, thought the admiral.

About ten minutes later, Penn sighted a very tiny image southbound of the horizon.

Penn: "HELMASMAN ... ALL SAILS... SOUTH COURSE."

The Admiral hurried down and ordered the flag captain to report to the rest of the expedition that he had sighted the missing boats, and they would to their rescue. He also ordered all other ships to follow their normal course. Penn knew he had to get a few miles closer because the captain of the other vessel did not have telescopes as powerful as his. The challenge would not be easy as the admiral's ship was going in the same course of the missing ships.

An hour later the boats were mutually visible, but the lost ships were not aware of the rescue and continued moving south.

The admiral gave the order to make noise to attract their attention. After some minutes, he realized that his strategy had worked; Penn saw with his powerful glasses that the ships had lowered sails to slow, and took a westbound course. A few minutes later they were able to communicate. The rescue was a success.

Penn and Venables in Barbados

The Windward Islands are a group of small islands in the northern part of the Lesser Antilles. Barbados is one of these islands, at 34 kilometers long and 23 kilometers wide, was discovered by the Portuguese explorer Pedro Campos in 1536. Campos was impressed by the large number of fig trees and hanging roots found on the islands. He called them "Os Barbados", meaning "the bearded", because of the resemblance of the fig trees to beards. After a short time, the Portuguese left the island because it lacked natural wealth, especially in precious metals. But the British had different ideas, and in 1627 the first British settlers arrived. The British already owned the nearby islands of St. Kitts (Saint Kitts) and Nevis (Nevis), and the new settlers were devoted to the cultivation of sugarcane using indigenous and African slaves. Over the next three decades the British converted the island into a prosperous sugar colony.

On January 26, 1655, the expedition of Penn and Venables arrived at Barbados. Admiral Penn ordered a review of all ships and to repair any damage and breakdowns. During the first weeks, groups were put to work in order to resupply the sailboats. At the same time, General Venables began a controversial recruitment of additional soldiers. According to his calculations, he needed to add about 3,000 men to the infantry force. These "soldiers" came not only from Barbados but also the adjacent islands, and they had no military training; rather they were former sailors, mercenaries and adventurers.

The practice and method of recruitment bothered Admiral Penn and Daniel Searle, governor of the island, but Venables continued his effort and said he had direct orders from the Protector.

Despite the strong confrontations, Penn and Venables met often to discuss details of the next step of the invasion. Since the end of February they had already agreed to maintain in absolute secret the decision about the first island to be attacked. Both Penn and Venables knew how much the first stage of the "Western Design" meant to Oliver Cromwell. This could not fail; it had to be a complete success.

Naval Battle against the pirates of the Caribbean

On March 3, General Venables decided to go for a tour of the Caribbean Sea as he wanted to become familiar with the new environment. He was not used to the warm temperatures of the tropics. The general was escorted by two smaller ships as he was not a sailor; he was an infantry man and knew little of navigation.

About noon they were close to the coast of the island of Nevis. At a distance the general saw four strange vessels that approached. General Venables asked his captain if he recognized the vessels' flag. The captain replied negatively, and ordered his flag captain to send the required identification to the approaching ships.

A few minutes passed and the four ships continued approaching. Now they could clearly distinguish that these were pirate ships; two of the boats were third class with about fifty guns each, the other two were small craft used by pirates to plunder at a smaller scale.

The wind was blowing in favor of the pirates; they were getting closer as the minutes passed. Pirates were excellent and very brave sailors as all they had done in their life was steal, loot and kidnap. Apparently the pirates thought that the general's vessels were carrying slaves.

The pirates were strategically placed alongside the English ships and began to bombard them. Previously Venables tried to leave the area, but the pirates were following very closely. The general ordered to counterattack. After about one hour of gunfire exchange, the pirates did not cease their incessant attack; they had established a serial shooting system on their opponents. One of Venables' ships had been seriously damaged and pirates were about to seize the ship. Pirates usually did not sink the ships in order to recover the loot or seize the boat.

One of the English ships had been seriously damaged and the pirates were attacking relentlessly when amid gunfire the central mast of one of the pirate ships fell into several pieces. The accurate guns of two English ships, which had arrived unnoticed, endlessly fired at the pirates' ships. The pirates were greatly perplexed and could not believe how those boats, even a little distance, could shoot so accurately.

The battle had taken a 180 degree turn; now the pirates tried to flee, but they could not. Penn's ships fired continuously until the pirates raised the white flag, signifying their defeat. The end result was an English ship severely damaged, but the pirates were defeated with a sunken ship and three captured.

The British returned to Barbados to repair the damage and recruit more soldiers or mercenaries because their next target for invasion would be La Española.

La Española, Hispaniola or the island of Santo Domingo

La Española, baptized with this name by Admiral Christopher Columbus on his first voyage, was discovered on December 5, 1492, and was part of a group of four islands in the Caribbean called Greater Antilles. Cuba, Jamaica and Puerto Rico complete the quartet.

At this earthly paradise the admiral marveled at the island; he was accustomed to the harsh cold climate of Genoa and Spain at this time of year. He wrote in his notes about the cool breeze and compared it with the air of Castile in April. He was also impressed by the flora and in his writings he spoke of green trees in winter. But perhaps what most touched the discoverer was the ingenuity, kindness and gentleness of the natives of the island, which he also described in several of his writings.

The best description of the first Spanish inhabitants is given by Juan Bosch in his book *Indian Historical Notes and Legends*, 1935. The professor says:

"Probably the Ciguayos took possession of the island before another race. Half-savage Indians,sloped forehead. At the beginning they were rough and bloodthirsty, they lived in caves and moved to the northern mountains, they must be short in numbers that would otherwise had resisted the Tainos, who came from the continent as peaceful conquerors. The Ciguayos were unfriendly warriors; they used the nightstick and the arrow and did not tolerate interference. The Tainos were farmers par excellence, dashing, beautiful, quiet. They adapted to the blessing of climate and began to soften some of the harsh customs they brought from the south.

In the decades preceding the discovery, some dark men, strong and fierce, bold look and aquiline nose, burst into the island, pushing the Tainos east and west, entering, as a wedge, finally they took possession of what is known today as the regions that correspond to the two provinces of Macoris, to Samana, in part, and the portion of Santo Domingo between the two provinces of Macoris: the Macorixes, belonging to the great family of the Caribs, will supplement the mosaic."

The first city in the Americas was founded by Christopher Columbus on January 2, 1493, and was named La Isabela in honor of Queen Isabella of Spain. This city was built on the north side of La Española, near what is today the city of Puerto Plata. In La Isabela the conquerors established the foundation for their headquarters. In this city they built the first town hall, the first military barracks, the first church, and the first seat of government of this new continent was founded. The people of La Isabela, after a while, founded the New Isabela (August 4, 1496) in the south-east of the mouth of the Ozama River. On August 4, 1502, Fray Nicolás de Obando founded the city of Santo Domingo de Guzmán in the south-west of the Ozama river bank, and it was populated by the inhabitants of the New Isabela, which had been destroyed by a hurricane.

During the following years the towns of Santiago de los Caballeros, La Vega, San Fernando de Montecristi, Puerto Plata and Higuey, among others, were founded. Santo Domingo had been developed more than all other cities of the time for several reasons: it was the seat of the colony's government authorities; it had an excellent seaport with a strategic location with direct access to major commercial sea lanes of the Caribbean Sea; it had natural protection against possible attacks by sea, and it had abundant sources of drinking water.

For the next few years Santo Domingo was in the cusp of America; to the point that in Europe, La Española was known as the Island of Santo Domingo. Extraordinary historical events happened during the next years.

From here Alonso de Ojeda went to conquer Venezuela in 1499; so did Diego Velázquez in 1511 to conquer Cuba, accompanied by Hernán Cortés, who later would do the same in Mexico. Francisco Pizarro and Diego de Almagro left for La Española to conquer Peru, and Juan Alvarado and Juan Ponce de León would conquer Guatemala and Puerto Rico respectively. Juan Ponce de León was the first European to visit Florida in search of the Fountain of Youth in 1513; that same year Vasco Nunez de Balboa, who discovered the Pacific Ocean, also went out from Santo Domingo.

On July 1526, an exploratory expedition led by Lucas Vazquez de Ayllon left the city of Puerto Plata accompanied by the missionaries Fray Anton de Montesinos and Pedro de Estrada. These missionaries achieved the historic feat of being the first Europeans to visit the Carolinas; these explorers laid the foundations for what is now considered the first religious temple in North America. Irish pilgrims came to America on the *Mayflower* in 1620, and Ayllon arrived in 1526. On September of that same year Vazquez de Ayllon, Estrada and Montesinos erected a cross near the river mouth at Jordan in North Carolina. In this place the first church was built in the United States of America, called the San Miguel Church.

We could go on telling other historical facts, but let's break for reflection on what Mr. Miguel Angel Rodriguez Pereyra says in his book *Esbozos de mi Patria* (Outline of my country) (Santo Domingo, 1978).

"Much has been said and written about the people of America. It is commendable and is very plausible for others. All of that deserves the most heartfelt gratitude to all who did it, as is known, the more you know about those people, the more we love those countries that one feels as if they were one's own. However, when speaking of all America and its history, you should think of this land of Santo Domingo, for being Hispaniola, La Española or Santo Domingo, or else Dominican Republic, the generating source of all existence, I believe, and that's the way it is, without Santo Domingo one can not speak about America, much less could write their history, for without Santo Domingo that history would not existed, neither tradition, custom, religion and language, because its genesis began in Santo Domingo and from here the culture was exported throughout the vast American territory."

While Santo Domingo became the capital of the New World, consequently there was a great demand for labor to construct new buildings, transport precious metals, cultivate land, and other needs required by the growth of emerging cities. As a result of this growing demand, the natives of the island were enslaved, cruelly persecuted, abused and humiliated by the new conquerors.

In 1502, the Commander Nicolás de Ovando ordered one of the most horrific crimes recorded in the history of America. It took place in Jaragua, where more than 300 Indians were killed including their chief Anacaona, who was sent to the gallows.

Such was the abuse the indigenous suffered that on December 21, 1511, Fray Anton de Montesinos delivered during a mass, where a number of Spanish authorities were present, the first clamor for justice in the New World. It was a cry of complaint and protest against the exploiters of Aborigines called the "Sermon on Advent", also known as the "Sermon of Montesinos". It reads:

"I am the voice of Christ crying out in the desert of this island, the most shocking and dangerous voice you have ever heard. You live and die in mortal sin for the cruelty and tyranny done against these innocent peoples. With what right and by which justice do you hold these Indians in such horrible servitude? By what authority do you carry out such detestable wars against the people of these lands – people so meek and peaceful? Are these not human beings? Do they not have rational souls? Are you not obliged to love them as yourselves? Do you not understand this? Do you not feel this? How can you be in such a profound and lethargic slumber? Be certain that in the state in which you find yourselves you can no more be saved than those who lack or have no faith in Jesus Christ."

The mistreatment of the indigenous people in 1520 is what is known as the reason for first uprising for freedom in America. A young Indian chief named Guarocuya, who had been educated by the Dominican Fathers and named Henry or Enriquillo, called for justice at the Royal Court, due the outrage that his wife was victim of a Spanish military. He was very frustrated because his demands were not taken into account, so he took up arms, accompanied by about 200 Indians, in the mountains of Bahoruco located in the southwestern part of the island. For about thirteen years he fought in the mountains against the executioners of the colony, for whom he caused significant casualties. Enriquillo knew very well the geography of the area. In 1533 he ended the insurrection and it was agreed that from that date the Indians would have the same rights as the Spanish, plus the allocation of an extensive territorial area that was called "Indian Reservation". The agreement was made between Guarocuya, representing the Aboriginal peoples and the Spanish Captain Francisco Barrionuevo who represented Europe's top authority at the time: Charles V of Spain and First Emperor of Germany.

The Indian reservation was a beautiful valley bordered to the west by hills, part of a great mountain chain where the tributaries of two rivers flows. To the east was a vast savannah, as flat as the palm of the hand, which led to a long bay washed by the warm waters of the Atlantic; while to the south was a rich forest of leafy trees, where ebony and mahogany were most abundant, and were surrounded by palm trees that stretched as far as the eye could see.

In this mesopotamia the indigenous had everything: abundant wild pigs in the mountains; sheep and cattle on the plains; wild birds such as turkeys, ducks, quail, doves, guineas and chickens; excellent farmland, watered by springs and streams; shrubs and an innumerable variety of fruit trees—all without the presence of ferocious animals. As if this were not enough, from the hills one could enjoy the splendor of an immense bay with the most beautiful beaches that human eyes have been able to contemplate. It was as if the Creator was inspired by this land to create his earthly paradise.

Two years after the Peace of Enriquillo, several small rebellions by African slaves took place on the island. The principal of these revolts was perpetrated in the southern part of La Española and was led by Lembá, the African, and the mulatto, Diego del Campo. After some agreements with the authorities, they settled in the same area just east close to Guarocuya. Mistreatment, abuse and humiliation at the hand of the Spaniards had been common and had inspired within those communities the warmth, affection and solidarity that reigned among its leaders.

The first manifestation of commerce between these cultures was a barter system, and the highest percentage of exchange took place between indigenous fishermen and the farmers from the east. Over time this exchange was also practiced frequently by marine adventurers, who came to the beaches to trade goods such as textiles, weapons, wines and perfumes in exchange for leather, wood, snuff, ginger, corn or cassava.

Indian Reservation and the town of Diego del Campo

They spent several decades there, and with the passing of time, the Indian Reservation and the town of Diego del Campo grew together, but each with the customs and culture of their ancestors. On the one hand, the Indians were extremely reserved— they practiced the concubinage among themselves to maintain an almost a pure race. Both men and women developed skills in using the bow and arrow; some were devoted to agriculture, growing corn, ginger and yucca (this root, after grinding and toasting was called cassava); while others were devoted to fishing, particularly women with impressive skills in underwater swimming. Most anglers could hold their breath under water for up to five minutes.

One activity that continued to be celebrated through the years was the "dance of cassava". This was a socio-religious celebration: at this event the people thank God for the good harvest. To commemorate this celebration they invited all people including residents of nearby villages, and the party lasted several days.

The first day was devoted to religious practices, while from the second day they enjoyed snuff smoking, many meals and many drinks. Almost everyone, men and women, got drunk.

The biggest attraction of the celebration consisted of dances and songs performed by specialized groups around large packages of cassava that had been previously packed in bags made from the fiber of a palmácea called "guano". The dances were very long and repetitive— some groups lasted up to eight hours of nonstop dancing— and the rhythmic chants were monotonous.

The residents of the town of Diego del Campo were devoted to farming and the cultivation of snuff, but specialized in horse riding and use of weapons. Many of them trained to launch a small knife or spear, called a "machete", up to three hundred yards and hit the target.

The African slaves who founded this community were polytheists and were gradually converted to Catholicism, but most continued believing in the religion of their ancestors, and from this mix came the belief known as "21 divisions" or "21 nations". This religious practice consists of 21 "mysteries", and each of these mysteries is executed by a divinity of African belief, which in turn is represented by a holy spiritual benefactor, archangel, or angel. Although each of the deities has many devotees in the Dominican Republic, the most popular are: Belie Belcan represented by "SAN MIGUEL", Ogun Balendjo "SAN SANTIAGO", Anaisa Pye "SANTA ANA", and Candelo "SAN CARLOS BORROMEO".

One popular activitiy of the inhabitants of the town of Diego del Campo is the "The stick holiday", which has traditionally been held to this day. In this festival, religious rites are held to honor the deities of the 21 divisions. Components of this celebration include dances and songs— either stanzas of religious origin or simply improvisations accompanied by the rhythmic sound of drums and gourds.

In 1653, Reliquiá became the leader of the Villa de Diego del Campo. He was a big man with very dark skin, had a huge force, could dominate a bull by its horns despite its nearly 300 pounds, was very agile, and stood at more than 6 feet tall.

The leader of the Indian Reservation was a tall burly man. His name was Guaroa, a brave Indian twenty-four years old, very expressive eyes, and straight black hair that hung to his shoulders. His name had been chosen by his father in honor of a former famous chieftain, the uncle of heroic warrior Enriquillo.

Guaroa's wife was Anaibis (daughter of a couple married to creole and Spanish). Her paternal grandmother was pure Indian. Anaibis was a beautiful woman, with clear eyes of amber to blue sky, her skin was tanned, and her straight black hair hung to her narrow waist. She had prominent breasts, shapely legs and sexy thighs, with hips as attractive as our imagination allows. It seems she lacked some ribs, but she had a lovely body, and looked like a goddess of Greek mythology.

Anaibis had a sweet look, and from her full lips came a voice that delighted the ears. This charming woman was gentle but of firm character. In her veins flowed, not only Spanish and African blood, but also the brave and indomitable Caribbean Indian blood.

Buccaneers, filibusters, Pirates and Corsairs

On September 1629, the Spanish attacked the Windward Islands of Saint Kitts and Nevis, with a fleet of thirty-five war ships. The vast majority of its inhabitants were French and English. Many assailants and Dutch adventurers escaped and took refuge in the unpopulated area located at the northwest end of La Española, near a small island called La Tortuga. Almost all new inhabitants were devoted to one of two types of activities: hunting wild cattle, which was plentiful at the time, or crime at sea. The first group adopted a sedentary lifestyle and established a trade to barter their leather. This group was called Buccaneers. It is believed that the origin of this word comes from "bucan", a name given to a device they used to roast meat.

The other group was made up of excellent sailors, former soldiers, mercenaries and adventurers who specialized in assault at sea but also practiced robbery and kidnapping on land. They divided their loot depending on the rank they occupied, and created their base of operations on Turtle Island. These thugs were called Filibusters. The origin of this word could be "flibustier", which is French for "assailant". As time passed these offenders were better known as pirates.

During the Middle Ages the monarchs granted the mayors official permission to attack enemy ships or populations. The permission document was known as "Letter of Marque" and its execution was very popular in developed countries of Europe during the fifteenth and sixteenth centuries.

The naval powers had granted the "Letter of Marque" to military, members of the nobility, wealthy individuals and private companies to conquer territories on behalf of the issuing country; the carriers of these patents were known as corsairs who, in most cases, acted as navigators licensed to pirate.

From the mid-sixteenth century and into the seventeenth, the Caribbean became a battleground where almost all conflicts that occurred between European powers were resolved— this is why some of the Antilles' islands changed motherland several times either, by treaty, convention or counter-invasions.

La Española was one of the most affected islands as it suffered numerous attacks by pirates like John Hawkins in 1565. But the most shocking attack occurred in 1586 when Francis Drake invaded the city of Santo Domingo where he kept kidnapped people for about a month, causing one of the most vile lootings in recorded history, all covered by the " Letter of Marque" given by Queen Elizabeth.

Over the next decades the island was attacked by pirates regularly, but it also was frequently attacked by buccaneers who penetrated the vicinity of the Cibao Valley, located in northwestern center of the island, looking for wild cows. All these activities kept the authorities of the island very busy. In order to defend the ground attacks by pirates and privateers, they created armed gangs composed of fifty skilled horsemen.

These groups were called "Fiftieth". But these efforts were not enough and the authorities were busy protecting other interests of higher priority, so it is not surprising that they neglected the population of the island of Santo Domingo. The Indian Reservation and the town of Diego del Campo were no exception— the Spanish rulers also forgot them.

Barlovento's Navy and pirate attacks

The Spanish galleons, loaded with gold from Mexico and Peru, had no choice but to make their journey to Spain via the waters of the Caribbean Sea. First the gold from Peru was transported overland across the Isthmus of Panama to the Atlantic, and from there the Spanish galleons began their trek through the Caribbean Sea and the Canal de la Mona.

Precious metals of Mexico were transported overland to be loaded and shipped by the Yucatan Channel to Havana, or one of the ports in northern La Española.

These routes were a great attraction for criminals of the sea. Continuous attacks and looting by pirates and privateers were becoming more frequent and intense to the point that by the mid-sixteenth century, the Spanish Crown needed to build new warships or modify some commercial ships in order to defend their overseas territories and secure the routes between Spain and its colonies. The Spanish government decided to build a fleet of well-armed vessels, with naval bases in the Spanish colonies in the Antilles arc. This war fleet was called Barlovento's Navy.

In early December 1653, four pirate boats approached the northeast coast of La Española, near the Indian Reservation and the town of Diego del Campo. The inhabitants of these colonies thought they were sailors looking to market, so they rushed to bring the goods to the barter points, but were surprised when two small boats began to disembark criminals and looters. Immediately the pirates, as usual, terrorized the villagers and quickly fear ensued in the community.

Guaroa, his wife Anaibis, and a group of Indians were hunting in the nearby hills. A boy of about twelve years of age who had escaped was able to inform them of what happened. Without delay the indigenous group came to the defense of the population. When they arrived to the town, many houses had been burned, screams of terror and disorder reigned everywhere, women and children ran away in desperation. Guaroa and his group had the advantage that they were on horseback and rode very well, and they soon began to fight the criminals, who battled with great skill.

Reliquiá sent reinforcements to help the fight against pirates, skilled in the use of bladed weapons. Melee fights broke out, with many deaths on both sides, but the natives managed to beat this group of offenders, while others, amid all the confusion, had escaped and kidnapped a group of women. Among the captives was Leilani, Anaibis' sister.

The pirates were ready to carry their victims and the booty to the ships waiting a short distance from the beach. Suddenly the sound of cannons was heard in the distance. A fleet of ten galleons from Barlovento's Navy approached, rapidly attacking the pirate ships, which immediately weighed anchor and tried to flee. The kidnappers were undecided whether to continue with their captives to the mother ships or to return ashore. One of the small boats decided to return to the beach; the other carrying the abducted women remained in the water.

This group of thugs were surprised by a handful of brave Indians with their accurate arrows who did not allow them to return— all pirates were killed. The other thugs decided to surrender and return ashore, where they were captured by the creoles who had joined the Indians.

After about four hours of fighting, the accurate shooting of the Spanish galleons managed to sink one of the boats and captured two others. After control of the situation at sea, the Spanish troops landed and arrested the pirates who had been ashore.

By the next day, several sailors and officers of the fleet had arrived, and for the first time ever three ethnic groups came together to celebrate. They enjoyed delicious food and danced to improvised melodies, harmonized with African's drums, Indians' gourds and the harmonics of the Spaniards— in short all celebrated the happy ending of a rescue that may have had a very unpleasant end.

One of the Starfleet officers of Barlovento's Navy called Darío García del Monte established a cordial relationship with the village leaders, especially with Guaroa and Leilani, his sister in law, with whom he was madly in love. Leilani, curiously maiden in her 20s, had similar feminine charms to those of her older sister. She liked to sing, and possessed a soprano voice. She had also been attracted to the young heartthrob Darío, who had promised to come back for her as soon as possible.

Island of Santo Domingo, February 1655

Since the mid-seventeenth century Spain had played down La Española and other West Indian possessions, as their wealth could not be compared to the substantial benefits produced by the colonies of Mexico, Cartagena and Peru. The Crown, to save resources, created a military institution called Captaincy General in order to govern the smaller colonies.

The Captain General was the highest military authority, yet exercised the functions of Civil Governor. In the late 1654s, the highest authority was exercised by the Spanish Juan Francisco Montemayor de Cuenca, Captain General of the island of Santo Domingo. But this title belonged to Don Bernardino de Meneses Bracamonte and Zapata, Count of Peñalva, who had been appointed Governor and Captain General of the island, but had not yet come to office.

Since early February 1655 the Spanish island authorities had been informed about the presence of the great English fleet on the island of Barbados. They also had knowledge of military power as well as recruitments conducted in the adjacent islands. These events indicate that an English attack of La Española was imminent.

The city of Santo Domingo was walled and protected by a few forts. The biggest ones were the Santa Barbara's Fort, located near the mouth of the Ozama River, and Fort San Geronimo, located on the southern coast of the Dominican Republic near what is now the Autonomous University of Santo Domingo.

Montemayor de Cuenca had at that time a garrison of about fifty armed men in the city of Santo Domingo and fifteen soldiers at Fort San Geronimo. The General Captain knew that it was virtually impossible to face the English military power with this force, so he organized an official emergency meeting. The meeting was attended by the Generals Damián del Castillo and Juan de Morfa and the young Lieutenant Dario Garcia del Monte; the latter had recently arrived after serving in the Barlovento's Navy. The meeting was extensive; they reviewed documents and irrefutable evidence that the great English invasion could occur anytime. After long hours of deliberation they agreed on the following strategy.

First: request reinforcements and weapons from the Captaincy General of the island of Puerto Rico.

Second: recruit men willing to face the Englishmen, but in a discreet manner so as not to alarm the population. The elderly still remembered the horrific attack that the English privateer Francis Drake perpetuated about forty years earlier.

Third: ask the officers from the "Fiftieth" to go to Santo Domingo as soon as possible. (The "Fiftieth" were groups of fifty skillful spearmen on horseback who defended the northern part of the colony from theft and looting by buccaneers and filibusters).

Fourth: to seek help from Guaroa and Reliquiá. This was the most controversial part of the strategy and was strongly opposed by Generals Del Castillo and De Morfa. They believed it was humiliating to ask for help from the indigenous and former slaves. However the young Lieutenant Dario Garcia, who had good legal skills, managed to convince the others, especially considering the danger they faced and the large numerical difference between the Spanish and the English.

Dario explained that about a year before, he had met Guaroa and Reliquiá in a clash with pirates. He exposed the great skill and good management of weapons by the Indians, especially the extraordinary skill with bows and arrows. He also emphasized the proper use of weapons by Reliquiá's men, and the courage with which they faced the enemies. We have no doubt that while the young lieutenant eloquently convinced the generals, he was also thinking about his reunion with Leilani.

That same day the Captain General contacted the missionary Fray Toledo Belarminio, a member of the Dominican Order who followed the principles and guidelines of Fray Bartolome de las Casas. (las Casas is considered one of the founders of modern international law as a champion of human rights and especially protector of Native Americans.)

Father Belarminio used to preach the gospel to the distant peoples who had no permanent priests. He was loved and respected, especially by the indigenous and ex-slaves.

The next day Lieutenant Darío García and the Toledo priest went to seek help from Guaroa and Reliquiá. It took a day on horseback; after arriving they rested, bathed and ate, and then met with leaders of both communities.

Father Belarminio explained in detail the dangerous situation that was facing La Española. He emphasized the dire consequences of an English invasion. Some ex-slaves expressed their rejection of any English or French rule as they had personally suffered the cruel abuses of slavery. The Spaniards had always treated the Africans more kindly, perhaps because they were never involved in the slave trade.

The discussions took hours. Guaroa was not convinced; he was very distrustful and thought he could be stripped of his land, so he adamantly opposed giving his support.

The Indian chief argued:

"How could they, after abuses and humiliation; abuses to us and to our ancestors, abuses from the Spanish. Now you come to ask for help? You forgot the killing of Jaragua and Anacaona? You forgot the crimes of Higuey and Saona? I remember, as a child, when they killed my grand uncle as a dog. No way! Don't count on me; furthermore, I do not trust the Spanish, they are a bunch of treacherous."

Lieutenant Darío García found it necessary to intervene; he had a big challenge ahead and could not return to Santo Domingo without success.

The young lieutenant made luxury eloquence, first said he understood why Guaroa disagreed while acknowledging the bad behavior of some of the conquerors, he stressed that some of the mentioned events had occurred over 150 years ago, now that belonged to the past; he also said that the Spaniards were not saints and that the treatment of Indians was very different from what had happened in previous years. He argued that any agreement would be respected in full as it was before a priest, said that he came on behalf of the highest authority, Juan Francisco Montemayor de Cuenca, Captain General of the Island, and finally he swore that he would expose his life to any betrayal. Darius paused, looked around, as if trying to guess the thoughts of those present, and not satisfied with the reaction he said.

"About a year ago I risked my life, when a group of cruel bandits looted with impunity and kidnapped a group of defenseless women. Those who want to invade us are from the same country as those pirates; they speak the same language as the pirates; they have the same religion as the pirates, AND THEY DO NOT BELIEVE IN THE HOLY. I assure you that they are as cruel, or worse than the group of murderers who we fought ourselves. Listen gentlemen, about five years ago the British fought a war in their own land, and killed over fifty thousand people among themselves. THOSE ARE THE SAME ENGLISH WHO WANT TO INVADE US. Do you imagine what they can do to us if they don't even respect their own blood line? Do you prefer that those bandits come and stripped your territories and to rape women? Do you prefer to go back to slavery? Or do you prefer to be governed by thieves who do not even speak our language?"

Darío was silent. The atmosphere became silent. All bowed their heads— no one dared to say a word. The questions had surprise them. Never before has anyone spoken so eloquently.

The skilful lieutenant maintained his firm stance watching everyone, but without looking at anyone. He knew he exaggerated his speech, but it was needed to achieve its objective.
Guaroa rose from his seat and broke the silence. He apologized and asked to speak with his five closest collaborators who had accompanied him to the meeting.

Among the chief's closest associates, was a man about sixty-five years old, who was highly respected by all citizens because he worked as a teacher— not only for children but he also taught adults. He was known by all as Don Onesimus.

Once gathered in the back of the house, Guaroa said:

"Don Onesimus, I would like to hear your advice before I make a decision, perhaps impulsive, which may be incorrect. Don Onesimus, what do you advise?"

Don Onesimus: "Guaroa, I've known you since you were born, and you know how much I respect you. I would never give you inappropriate advice. After carefully listening to Lieutenant Dario Garcia, who I think is a serious man, I began to reflect on the saying: "better the devil you know than the devil you don't". While it is true that the Spaniards have done a lot of damage to us, we already know them and they have not bothered us lately. Those who are to come, we don't know at all what they will do with us. They don't even speak our language. I think we should unite and fight against those who want to invade us. But you are the leader, whatever you decide we will back you up."

The chief was thoughtful and after a few seconds he asked the four remaining partners for their opinions. All expressed briefly that they were in total agreement with Don Onesimus.

Guaroa and the group returned to the meeting, where all anxiously awaited the Cacique's response. He explained that their forces would rally to the defense of Santo Domingo, but on one condition: the agreement had to be carried out under an Indian oath between Reliquiá, Father Belarminio, Lieutenant Dario Garcia and Guaroa.

According to custom, the "Indian oath" had to be made on a hill after the first cockcrowing before sunrise.

Indian Oath

That same night, with a full moon in the sky, Guaroa had invited five of his closest collaborators. Reliquiá had done the same. They went to a nearby hill, built a campfire and sat down around it. They were accompanied by the peculiar sounds of night insects, conversation, jokes and occasional laughter. Fresh winds blew slightly, while in the distance they could see the extraordinary beauty of the peninsula. They slept very little after talking all night, smoking snuff and drinking ginger tea. Only father Belarminio had fallen asleep and snored like a dormouse.

Reliquiá had participated in such an oath a few years earlier. He had agreed with Guaroa that an attack on one of the populations would be considered an offense to both villages; however, Darío and the priest had no idea what would happen. Reliquiá remained serene; he had taken several shots of rum which he had brought in a small bottle and joked occasionally.

It was roughly about four in the morning when the first crowing of a rooster was heard in the distance. Guaroa stood up and walked around the campfire. He was serious-minded, and wore typical Indian clothes. His gaze fixed on the horizon, his eyes unblinking; he seemed like a different person. Everyone else got to their feet and formed a circle. The chief raised his arms, forming an X and looking toward heaven, and he said in an inspired voice:

"We have respected for hundreds of years our principles and commandments of our indigenous gods who said DO NOT LIE, DO NOT BE LAZY, DO NOT STEAL and RESPECT THE ELDERLY"

Reliquiá raised his arms in the form of X, approached the chief and at the same time invited the priest and the lieutenant to do the same.

Guaroa: "In the eyes of all the gods of the universe, we swear tonight to defend our island, even with our lives if necessary, from the invasion of the British or any other nation."

Reliquiá, the lieutenant and the priest repeated the same.

Guaroa "We swear non betrayal between us, and to uphold mutual defense from future attacks."

Reliquiá, the lieutenant and the priest repeated the same.

Guaroa: "This oath is valid with the seal of our blood."

Reliquiá, the lieutenant and the priest repeated the same.

Guaroa drew a sharp knife and made a small wound on the side of his right bicep, then he handed the knife to Reliquiá who did the same. The priest was shaking, the lieutenant was firm but nervous— they could not believe what was going on. After a few seconds they also made small wounds with the knife.

The Indian chief approached in turn Reliquiá, the priest and finally the lieutenant. With each one he rubbed his bloody biceps; the ceremony continued until all had done the same. They crossed their forearms— perhaps symbolizing the strength of the union. For about two minutes they stood in silence, with their eyes closed and their heads lifted to heaven.

Guaroa: "Gods of heaven, I'm not sure if I made the right decision for my people, but I think it is better the devil you know than the devil you don't. I assure you, my gods, that I still do not trust the Spaniards after all they have done to us, and I swear, my gods, if the Spanish betray us or deceive us again, I will fight with all the fury of my heart and I will not stop no matter what. I swear by all my forefathers."

Reliquiá: "San Miguel, I've never been religious, but I've always been your faithful devotee, San Miguel, San Miguel, I beg you to guide me to the right path. San Miguel, I know I made the right decision. San Miguel, my grandparents always told me how badly they were treated when they were slaves of the French or English. San Miguel, these English are the most evil men on the face of the earth. They are the ones who come to attack. San Miguel, they are a bunch of mother... I'm sorry, San Miguel, forgive me. I promise, San Miguel, that if we are victorious I will pray to you every day, I swear to you, San Miguel."

Lieutenant Garcia: "Listen Lord, I have participated in many battles. Lord, I killed people during combat, forgive me if I have sinned. I pray you will protect all of us: whites, Indians, blacks, women, children, military, all without exception. I am committed to these people to join hands to fight against a strong enemy. I will fulfill my promise, but I ask you, Lord, do not leave us— right now more than ever we need your help. Protect us, Lord."

Father Belarminio: "Lord Heavenly Father, I apologize because I have been a sinner, I mean to sin by the oath in which I participated. I ask your forgiveness, Lord, I could not find another way to protect my flock from the demonized enemy that lurks. I beg for your divine protection— you are the only one who can save us from the serious danger looming before us. Please give us strength and courage to face the terrible enemy that we will encounter. I pray you, in the name of the Father, the Son and the Holy Spirit, Amen."

After several minutes of silence, Guaroa was the first to loosen from the two people beside him. The ceremony was over. All of them slowly walked down the hill and headed home.

The priest and the lieutenant went to the chief's house, took a break, then left for Santo Domingo.

INVASION BY PENN AND VENABLES

Friday, April 23, 1655

Early in the morning, the Captain General of La Española, Francisco Montemayor de Cuenca, was informed of the presence of fifty-six warships of the British navy on the coast of Santo Domingo, in what is now known as the Pleasure of Studies. Penn and Venables had sailed from Barbados and, after recruiting additional troops in Saint Kitts and Nevis, they crossed the Mona Passage and reached La Española with 12,800 men and 150 horses.

Montemayor de Cuenca ordered patrols throughout the city, and urgently sent an emissary to ask for reinforcements from Guaroa and Reliquiá.

By this time 200 soldiers and weapons had arrived from Puerto Rico, and 400 skilled lancers of the "Fiftieth" from Santiago de los Caballeros and La Vega.

Over the past two days, strong winds and violent waves had upset Admiral Penn, who did not know the geography of the area well and did not know that the beaches near Santo Domingo were not very deep. This did not allow him to get too close to the coast; however, he stood watching from atop his lookout, with his powerful telescopes, for other possible avenues of approach or landing.

Penn's idea was to land the bulk of the infantry not too far from its target in order to carry out a massive attack on the city. It was extremely important to the admiral to know the exact location of the ground troops, because part of his plan of attack was to bombard the city before the landing of troops. Also by using this strategy he could gain better control of the enemy's communication and the troop's supplies.

Venables did not share this idea as he felt that the ground attack should be carried out from two opposing fronts and therefore two landing points would be required, each with about fifteen support vessels. The general insisted that through a two-pronged attack on the enemy, they would have to divide their defenses and this would favor their infantry.
Venables had knowledge of his opponent's weaknesses, most notably the number of soldiers in the Spanish infantry, thus assuring that his troops would take the city in three days without using the ships' guns. The difference in attack tactics caused a heated argument between the two generals, but in the end Admiral Penn was convinced that the Venables' strategy, from the military point of view, was the best option.

Saturday, April 24

In and around the city of Santo Domingo, a spectacular day dawned, the sky was completely clear, and a breeze gently blew from the northeast. Very early in the morning Admiral Penn went out in a small boat to personally explore the surroundings to find a possible landing beach. The ideal location needed to meet the following requirements:

1. Close to sources of drinking water.

2. Beach or natural harbor to facilitate the landing of troops.

3. Suitable land for the establishment of a war camp.

At the Indian reservation, at approximately ten a.m., Guaroa was ready to go to the defense of Santo Domingo. The previous day, he had contacted his followers and had 400 skilled warriors with their respective horses, who were well armed— many had muskets acquired by smuggling. Anaibis and Leilani were also in the group, mounted on two beautiful black horses. The ladies had requested permission to participate in the adventure. The cacique initially refused, but they insisted, arguing that they had a debt with Lieutenant Dario Garcia because he saved Leilani's life.

After much pleading and insistence Guaroa relented; he knew the potential of these two women. They handled the bow and arrow better than any man, were expert swimmers, and were as brave as their Carib Indians descendants.

Reliquiá left two hours later with 500 men on horses; most of them had muskets, the others were armed with spears, machetes and knives. Most of these Creoles were descendants of African slaves and were accustomed to spending whole days outdoors and could survive in the Caribbean's worst weather. These warriors were extremely skillful and brave. Some legends of the population said that five of them could face 100 men and be victorious.

By late afternoon, Admiral Penn had returned to his ship. *Second Class Swiftsure* had become commander of the invasion, and he immediately met with General Venables, Vice Admiral William Goodson, Captain-Flag, Jonas Poole and a few infantry officers. At this meeting they chose the geographical points for landing the invading troops, with supplies for a week. They also agreed on a set war strategy that would continue for the next few days.

Sunday, April 25

Early in the morning, at the mouth of the Ozama River, near today's port of Haina in Santo Domingo, 3,000 British soldiers landed with 20 horses for senior officers. Six thousand soldiers and 80 horses entered the Nizao's river mouth, located on the south coast of the Dominican Republic about 60 kilometers west of the city of Santo Domingo.

At about nine o'clock, Guaroa and Reliquiá's reinforcements arrived at Santo Domingo. They were greeted by Father Belarminio and Lieutenant Dario Garcia who led them to the office of General Fuentemayor, where they were informed of the situation of war in the city.

The priest invited Leilani, who was excellent singer, to accompany the church choir to a special mass to be held that Sunday before sunset at the Cathedral of America. (This impressive temple, whose original name was Basilica Santa Maria la Menor, took 20 years to build and the opening took place in 1541.) The religious ceremony began at about five p.m., and most of the population had gathered to pray for the welfare of the people, the church was completely full, civil and military personalities were present: among others, General Fuentemayor de Cuenca and his wife, Guaroa, Anaibis, Reliquiá and Lieutenant Dario Garcia.

The priest addressed the congregation, he read and talked about the gospel, but he never mentioned the critical situation they were in, not wanting to alarm the population, but he did express words of fellowship, encouragement and hope.

During communion the choir, accompanied by Leilani and a nun who masterfully played the organ, sang the Ave Maria. The voice of the soprano Leilani sounded with great intensity, helped by the temple's good acoustics. A voice like Leilani's had never been heard in the temple: the intonation and affinity was perfect, and the audience was stunned— it was though an angel sang from heaven.

Monday, April 26

Much of the invading troops were militarily undisciplined people: many of the "soldiers" were confused and did not know who their bosses were. Since the landing there had been some conflict, disobediences and disorganization, and the infantry personnel were demoralized by the presence of immoral mercenaries whose only interest was money.

Early in the morning at the Nizao's river camp, an English officer arrived with three soldiers to explore the vicinity, as naturally he had little knowledge of the geography of the area.

After a two-hour tour, the officer left the group and was lost, disoriented in the bush, and by ill luck he fell prey to one of General Fuentemayor's officers. After extensive questioning, the English officer gave a full report on the location and number of invaders that were on the island.

Tuesday, April 27

A tropical wave hit, with heavy rains and winds across the south— east of La Española. Torrential rains fell on the city all day, with thunder and lightning predicting more stormy days ahead. Due to the weather conditions, the invaders remained guarded in their war camps; however, Guaroa and Relic gathered his men and outlined strategies to follow as soon as weather conditions allowed. His men, like all Caribbean warriors, were used to fighting in adverse conditions and could survive the weather.

Wednesday, April 28

One hundred lancers of the "Fiftieth" and one hundred of Reliquiá men went out to meet the invading troops that had landed by Haina. Another group of armed men went out to San Geronimo's fort, which was halfway between Haina and the city of Santo Domingo.

Similarly, Guaroa directed one hundred of his men toward the mouth of the Nizao river, where the more distant enemy camp was located. The chief was aware of the numerical superiority of his opponents, so he had chosen to attack by surprise since he now knew the exact location of the English camp. At about eight o'clock in the evening, when the British least expected, they were attacked with silent, but aimed arrows shot out from the darkness. The attack lasted about forty minutes: the English had no idea where the enemy came from, and the attack ensued disorder. Some were shouting, "We are being attacked", "Take up arms", their faces filled with terror. Suddenly the horses galloped away. The night was dark and the ground was still wet from the previous day's rain, limiting ground movement, to the distress of the soldiers. The British were able to relieve some of their wounded. At dawn the invaders found many dead everywhere; it was an extremely fast attack, but devastating. An English officer sent a small boat to inform Penn and Venables what had happened.

Thursday, April 29

The warriors of the "Fiftieth" rose early and headed towards the English war camp of Haina Reliquiá had agreed to protect the rear.

The clock struck nine o'clock when one of the captains of the "Fiftieth" saw a column of about 1,000 British soldiers on their way to the city of Santo Domingo; some officers rode horses, as did all the Creoles.

At about ten o'clock the first encounter between the English invaders and the "Fiftieth" lancers occurred. The brave and courageous lancers fiercely attacked the British, who had never before faced soldiers that made war with such skill and tenacity. It was a fierce battle; the British had the advantage to outnumber the Creoles, but the Creoles were more skilled and fought more effectively. After about thirty minutes of combat, Reliquiá suddenly appeared with his imposing figure leading his five hundred warriors and came tenaciously upon against the English. The English could not handle the onslaught and chose to flee in terror. Almost all the English were killed, several wounded, very few escaped. The Creoles suffered few casualties and very few wounded.

Friday, April 30

Both Penn and Venables, since before the invasion, believed that Spanish forces would surrender without resistance, once they witnessed the magnitude of the English infantry. However, in light of the strong attack against thr British troops, Admiral Penn decided to change tactics of attack and called for an emergency meeting with General Venables and several officers.

The meeting took about two hours and resulted in a new invasion plan. Ten ships would approach as close as possible to bombard Santo Domingo, and after this attack ground troops from Haina and Nizao would move en masse to take the city.
For about twelve hours the British cannons did not stop shooting, but fortunately few bullets achieved their goal; not even the powerful guns fore and aft got there. The British ships were too far from the city; however, this intimidated much of the population, who left their belongings and ran to the surrounding fields.

This new strategic failure was extremely worrying for Penn and General Venables, who never before in their military careers had experienced so many frustrating events.

Saturday, May 1

Early the next morning, Guaroa, Reliquiá and Lieutenant Dario Garcia met to plot the next surprise attack against the invading forces. Guaroa explained that on the night of the previous attack he was able to see three small boats transporting supplies, and at the same time to communicate amongst the troops. The chief said that it would be a blow to the enemy if they could disable these vessels, and to that end he developed a plan. His strategy was to get as close as possible to the boats and launch flaming arrows, but to do that they had to swim across a small bay where the ships were guarded. After some discussion it was agreed that Guaroa would carry out the plan.

Early that night, Guaroa, Reliquiá, Anaibis and Leilani went out the city, accompanied by some fifty heavily armed men. Later that night, when it was very dark indeed, they began to execute their plan. They were about a mile from the ships, which were anchored near the English war camp but sheltered by high cliffs. The only way to sabotage the ships was to swim.

Only Anaibis or Leilani were able to make the crossing, but this was part of the plan. Both women entered the water, carrying bows, arrows and fuel in tightly closed bottles. It took about twenty minutes in the water and they approached the boats without being spotted. Only two sailors watched the boats. They quietly fired flaming arrows at each of the ships; the guards must have been asleep because it took several minutes before the calls for help were heard, but it was too late. The three ships were burning brightly, and there was no time to receive help from the soldiers at the camp. While this was happening the bold women returned to the shore where Guaroa, Reliquiá and the others waited.

Sunday, May 2

Between Santo Domingo and Haina was a fort strong called San Geronimo. This fort was built to protect the city from privateers' attacks like the one conducted in 1586 by the English privateer Francis Drake.

The fort was under the command of General Damián del Castillo and the general had about fifty regular soldiers, but the over previous days this had increased to about two hundred additional Creoles trained to fight alongside their "Fiftieth", the filibusters thieves of the north of the island.

At about eleven in the morning one of the guards on horseback approached the fort's gate and informed the General Del Castillo that a large column of British soldiers was on the way. The general sent to inform the Captain General Fuentemayor of the impending attack.

From midday the sky grew darker until it was completely covered with gray clouds and heavy rain, causing the invading troops to stop their advance.

Monday, May 3

The day was cloudless, the sun shone brightly, and British troops had resumed the advance to Fort San Geronimo.

At about ten in the morning the invading forces were near the fort, but their first attempt at invasion was repelled by the Creoles. The British returned to their original position and waited expectantly; apparently this was an attack to "take the pulse" of resistance.

At about eleven, another attempt to take the fort occurred, and this time the troops were more numerous and aggressive. The Creoles fought back; heroically, however this time they suffered heavy casualties. Apparently the British officers' plan consisted of sporadic attacks to inflict casualties slowly until they surrendered.

Another attack, this time with the whole bulk of the British troops, occurred at about one in the afternoon. The English officers had decided to gamble everything on the attack and was very fierce. The sheer number of invaders caused heavy casualties to the Creoles.

The fortress was just about to be taken by the British troops, when a strong contingent arrived led by General Juan de Morfa and accompanied by Lieutenant Dario Garcia and Guaroa and Reliquiá's men. They all arrived on horseback and began the bloodiest battle recorded so far in the history of the Dominican Republic.

Although Spanish and native defenders had many casualties, the aggression and skill of the enraged Creoles caused many casualties for the enemy. The battlefield looked like a scene from a Dantesque work: a lot of blood, many dead horses, and mutilated human bodies everywhere.

Given this surprising and devastating counter-attack, the remaining invaders had no choise but to abandon the attack and run desperately to "save face".

Tuesday, May 4

British troops were surprised by the Creoles' unexpected resistance, and the invaders were very demoralized by the great losses. Many soldiers were willing to surrender before engaging in another battle, including some officers that secretly shared this idea.

Many mistakes were made in the way that the invasion was organized; one of those mistakes was the landing at the Nizao river mouth, because this point was far from the city of Santo Domingo. In addition, the disorganization and demoralization of infantry personnel, the poor food and quality of drinking water caused many English soldiers to get sick. The severe tropical weather, especially the rain and warmth of May, caused a large number of invaders to suffer from malaria.

To all this must be added that, according to legend, the British soldiers were terrified of crabs and the luminescent insects of the tropics.

In just nine days the British invading forces had losses of 2,500 soldiers killed and 800 wounded, sick or missing; Penn and Venables had lost nearly a third of their infantry on the ground.

At about one in the afternoon. Penn and Venables got together and made the decision to send a few small vessels to pick up all the invading troops who were left in the camps of Haina and Nizao.

Wednesday, May 5

Early in the morning Penn and Venables' naval armada weighed anchor and moved away from the coast of Santo Domingo. The military or the new navy of the Protector Oliver Cromwell had never before been defeated.

The Spaniards, Indians and Creoles of Santo Domingo had defeated the most powerful navy of the universe.

EPILOGUE

It is fair to acknowledge the extraordinary historical contribution made by the heroic fighters who defeated the English army in Penn and Venables' invasion. If La Española had fallen to the British, it's likely that all other conquests on Cromwell's agenda would had been achieved, in a domino effect of conquests.

With the occupation of the island of Santo Domingo, the Protector had established his first headquarters of heavily armed groups on the island, then had continued with the other Greater Antilles, which had assured him control of the Caribbean's seaways. Consequently the conquest of the colony of Cartagena, the Viceroyalty of Peru and the Mexican Empire had been a manageable issue through good military strategies.

Without the victory of Spaniards and Creoles against Penn and Venables, the American continent's history would be different: the official language of most Latin American countries would be English. Maybe Miguel Hidalgo and Costilla would not have launched the war-cry, "Grito de Dolores" in Mexico, or perhaps Simon Bolivar would never have liberated five South American countries. Imagine Quisqueya without Duarte, Cuba without Martí or Thomas Jefferson without having the opportunity to announce on July 4, 1776, the Declaration of Independence of the United States of America.

The author

GENERAL BIBLIOGRAPHY

Ashley, Maurice, *Cromwell*, Prentice-Hall Inc., New Jersey, USA, 1969.

Bosch, Juan. Obras Completas. *Narrativa Tomo I, Indios Apuntes Históricos y Leyendas. Textos Histórico-Sociales Tomo V*. Editora Corripio CxA, Santo Domingo, RD, 1991.

Durant, Will and Ariel, *The Story of Civilization*, The Age of Louis XIV, Simon and Schuster, New York, 1963

Fraser, Antonia. *Cromwell: The Lord Protector*. Alfred A. Knopf Inc. New York, USA, 1973.

Moya Pons, Frank, *Manual de Historia Dominicana*. Editora Buho, C x A, Santo Domingo, RD, 2008

Peguero, Valentina y De los Santos, Danilo. *Visión General de la Historia Dominicana*. Editora Corripio CxA, Santo Domingo, RD, 1983.

Rodríguez Pereyra, Miguel Angel. *Esbozos de mi Patria*, Conceptos Históricos. Editora Educativa Dominicana, Santiago, RD, 1978.

Wedgwood, CV, *Oliver Cromwell*. Barns & Noble Books, USA, 1994.